W9-CFR-077

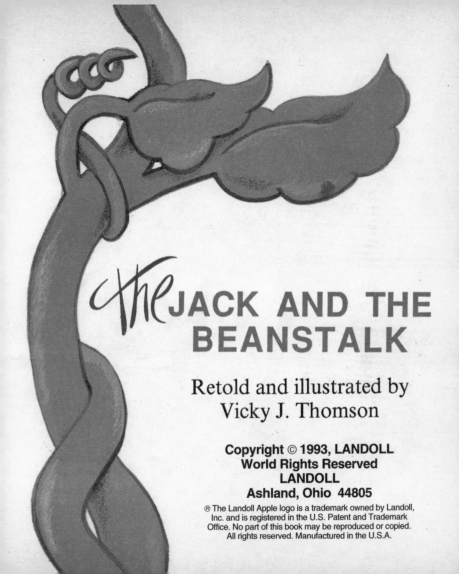

the JACK AND THE BEANSTALK

Retold and illustrated by
Vicky J. Thomson

Copyright © 1993, LANDOLL
World Rights Reserved
LANDOLL
Ashland, Ohio 44805

® The Landoll Apple logo is a trademark owned by Landoll,
Inc. and is registered in the U.S. Patent and Trademark
Office. No part of this book may be reproduced or copied.
All rights reserved. Manufactured in the U.S.A.

Long ago, there was a poor
widow who lived with her son,
Jack.

One day she told him, "Once,
until a giant came and took her,
we had a goose that laid golden
eggs. Now we have no money,
so you must take the cow to
market and sell her."

The next day, on his way to market, Jack met an odd man.

"Where are you taking your fine cow?" he asked.

"I'm taking her to sell at market," answered Jack.

"Wouldn't you like these magic beans in exchange for your cow?" he asked.

Jack thought
magic beans
would be a
fine bargain
and gladly
gave the
man the cow.

He hurried
home to tell
his mother
about the
magic beans.

When his mother asked how much money he had gotten for the cow, Jack showed her the magic beans.

"Magic beans. You foolish boy," she cried as she threw the beans out the window.

The next morning, Jack ran to the window. The magic beans had grown into a giant beanstalk!

Jack hurried outside
and began to climb
the beanstalk.

As Jack reached the top, he saw a castle in the distance and started towards it.

Jack walked
bravely to
the castle
and slowly
pushed open
the door.
There stood
a kind-looking
woman.

"Come in boy," she said, "Just beware of my husband, the giant."

The kind woman cooked Jack supper.
But, just as he sat to eat, he heard
a loud THUMP! THUMP! THUMP!

"My husband, the giant, is coming,"
she cried, "Quickly, hide in the
basket!"

"Fee! Fi! Fo! Fum!" the giant bellowed as he tromped into the room, "I smell someone hiding in my castle!"

"Nonsense!" laughed the woman, "It is only your supper. Now sit and eat."

After he had finished, the giant yelled, "Bring me the goose!"

"Lay!" he ordered the goose, and she laid a golden egg.

"Our goose the giant stole from us!" thought Jack.

Over and over, the giant ordered the goose to lay eggs. Soon, the giant fell fast asleep. Quickly, Jack climbed out of the basket and picked up the magic goose. The startled goose began to honk loudly and woke the snoring giant.

With the goose tucked under his arm, Jack ran as fast as he could out of the castle.

With the giant
running after
him, Jack ran
to the beanstalk
and began to
slide down.

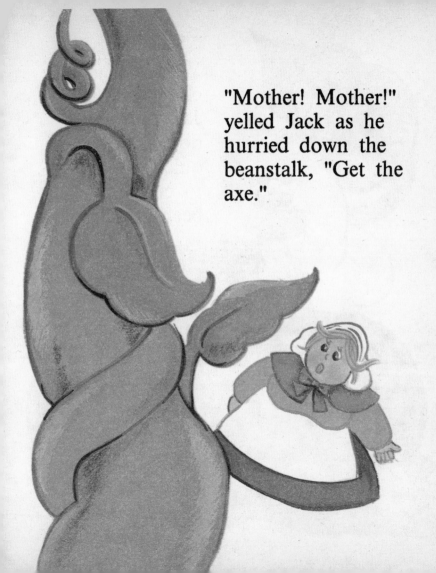

"Mother! Mother!" yelled Jack as he hurried down the beanstalk, "Get the axe."

With the giant
close behind,
Jack jumped
down and
quickly began
to cut the
beanstalk.

With a thunderous roar, the giant
and beanstalk came crashing to
the ground. Jack told his mother
all that had happened.

The magic goose continued to lay
golden eggs and Jack and his
mother lived happily ever after.